# Rock Springs Weddings

Kaci M. Rose

Five Little Roses Publishing

Copyright © 2020, by Kaci M. Rose via Five Little Roses Publishing. All Rights Reserved.

No part of this publication may be reproduced, distributed, or transmitted in any form or by any means, including photocopying, recording, or other electronic or mechanical methods, or by any information storage and retrieval system without the prior written permission of the publisher, except in the case of very brief quotations embodied in critical reviews and certain other noncommercial uses permitted by copyright law.

Publisher's Note: This is a work of fiction. Names, characters, places, and incidents are a product of the author's imagination. Locales and public names are sometimes used for atmospheric purposes. Any resemblance to actual people, living or dead, or to businesses, companies, events, institutions, or locales is completely coincidental.

Book Cover By: **Sarah Kil Creative Studio**

Editing By: Anna @ Indie Hub

# Contents

| | |
|---|---|
| Get Free Books! | VII |
| 1. Chapter 1 | 1 |
| 2. Chapter 2 | 11 |
| 3. Chapter 3 | 19 |
| 4. Chapter 4 | 29 |
| 5. Chapter 5 | 35 |
| 6. Chapter 6 | 45 |
| 7. Chapter 7 | 51 |
| 8. Chapter 8 | 61 |
| 9. Chapter 9 | 69 |
| 10. Chapter 10 | 77 |
| 11. Wedding Bonus Chapter | 87 |
| More Books by Kaci M. Rose | 95 |

| | |
|---|---|
| Connect with Kaci M. Rose | 97 |
| About Kaci M Rose | 99 |
| Please Leave a Review! | 101 |

# Get Free Books!

Would you like some free cowboy books? **If you join Kaci M. Rose's Newsletter you get books and bonus epilogues free! Join Kaci M. Rose's newsletter and get your free books!**
https://www.kacirose.com/KMR-Newsletter

**Now on to the story!**

# Chapter 1

## Riley

I can't believe I'm getting married today. We've been holed up in Sage's room getting ready. She insisted we used hers because it's bigger. I agreed because I love her room, and what with it being where my story on the ranch began, it felt for this chapter to start here too.

I can't help but laugh though when she ducks out while we are amid-preparations.

"Well looks like Colt couldn't wait any longer to see her," Megan says with a laugh.

"Can't blame the guy." I sigh. "I'm so ready to see Blaze."

"I bet." Megan smiles and sits down on the couch.

At the thought of seeing Blaze, my future husband, my stomach flutters, and I place my hand over it as I smile. I just found out I'm pregnant. I haven't told anyone. Not even Blaze.

He's given me so much, I can't wait to share the news with him. I know he can't wait to start a family, he's been dropping hints long enough now for me to know it's his biggest dream. I've been thinking all day of how to tell him, but I think I will let the day play out and tell him once we are alone after the reception. *But* if a good time presents itself, I might do it beforehand.

Sage comes back with her hair just a little out of place and giggles when Megan comments on it. As Megan fixes her hair, I just take them in. I didn't think a life like this was possible with sisters who are my best friends and a family who loves me with everything they have.

"The guys are getting ready to head outside. Colt is getting Blaze in place to do the pictures at the corner of the barn," Sage tells us.

When Sage looks at me her face falls. "What's wrong? Are you having second thoughts? I can sneak you out of here. My offer to take you to Alaska still stands."

"No that's not it. It's just hit me that my mom and dad aren't here. I knew they wouldn't be. I guess I just didn't expect it to hit me so hard. You know, no pictures, none of my dad walking me down the aisle." I try to shrug it off as I take a deep breath, now is not the time to break down.

Sage walks over and hugs me. "It's okay. Weddings bring out weird emotions. Do we need to take a minute?"

"No, let's get moving, distract me."

We are going to do a few photos of Blaze standing at the back of the barn at one corner and reaching around the corner to hold my hand. He won't be able to see me, but the camera will get both of us. I saw the idea on a wedding website and fell in love with it. It was the one thing I knew we had to have at the wedding.

The barn has played such a huge part in our relationship and my journey to where I am. It's where Blaze found me when we met for the first time. It is also where he proposed.

Sage, Megan, and I make our way downstairs and the girls get me in position for the photos. As soon as Blaze takes my hand, my nerves settle.

"Hey, baby." His deep voice washes over me.

"Blaze." I sigh, causing him to chuckle.

"Less than an hour and I get to watch you walk down the aisle. Riley baby, I can't wait."

"I can't either. I wish I'd thought to get married earlier in the day. Time is dragging on."

"It is, but after today we don't have to be apart again. I missed having you in my arms last night." There's a pout in his voice which makes me grin.

We get called to smile at the camera and I think about last night. Sage insisted I stay in her room because Blaze couldn't see me after midnight. We texted for hours though, neither of us able to sleep without the other.

Once the photos are done, Blaze squeezes my hand. "I love you, Riley."

"I love you too, Blaze."

The girls whisk me back into the house for some more pictures before it's finally time to head to the barn. Megan sent me pictures earlier today of the barn as they were decorating it. I love how it's turned out.

The walkway to the barn is lined in lanterns, at the doorway, there are a bunch of hanging twinkle lights forming a curtain for me to walk through.

We aren't having a lot of people there or a long ceremony so instead of chairs we are setting up bales of hay and covering them with blankets. I wanted to keep it very rustic and true to how we met. It may not have been the best time in my life, but meeting Blaze was the best thing to ever happen to me. So when Megan said she had a surprise with the decorations and asked me to trust her, I went with it. The most important part is that I'm marrying Blaze.

As everyone starts making their way out the side door to the barn Blaze's dad, Tim steps up to me.

"I don't want to overstep but Sage texted me saying you were upset your dad wasn't here to walk you down the aisle. I'm a poor stand in, but I'd be honored if you'd allow me to fill in."

I wrap him in a huge hug. "Thank you. That would mean everything," I whisper in his ear.

We slowly make our way to the barn and when we step through the curtain of lights I gasp. Megan and strung more fairy lights across the aisle from one side of the hayloft to the other all the way down to where Blaze is standing.

When my eyes land on Blaze everything else fades away, all my worries and burdens are gone, my emotions calm like water on a still lake.

I think of the little secret I have for him. Our little life we are going to bring into this world.

Blaze is standing at the end of the aisle with a look full of love for me on his face. He's in his cowboy formal, a casual suit, cowboy boots, and a cowboy hat. He looks so damn sexy I want to pull him out of here and back to bed, and not leave it for a week. It must be pregnancy hormones. I read they can make women horny.

I'm about halfway up the aisle when Blaze looks down at his feet for a brief moment. When he looks back up there are tears swimming in his eyes. I know he is trying to get his emotions in check. That does something to a girl when you see what much emotion in the man you are about to marry.

Butterflies erupt in my stomach as we get closer and I know it's way too early for me to feel the little life we created, but I like to think he or she is making themselves known.

Tim puts my hand into Blaze's and Pastor Greg starts the ceremony. I don't hear or see anything because I can't take my eyes off Blaze. We say our vows and exchange our rings and before I know it it's time for our kiss.

Blaze pulls me in close and runs his thumb over my lower lip as pulls me into him.

"You look absolutely beautiful today, Riley."

"You look pretty handsome yourself there, cowboy."

That causes him to smile as he leans down to kiss me. Our first kiss as husband and wife. This kiss feels different. It feels more important, sexier, and better than any kiss before it. Blaze must feel it too because he pulls away with a soft moan.

He has a huge smile on his face, and he takes my hand and walks me back down the aisle to everyone cheering. We head to his truck for a few minutes to ourselves before we head out for photos.

# Chapter 2

I think I am still in shock. I just found out Riley is pregnant. The whole place is a buzz and Mom hasn't left her side. Mom has been bugging us for Grandbabies and I know this is a dream come true for her.

I want nothing more than to pull Riley from here and be alone, but I want her to have this moment too. Our family and friends rally around her, showing her the love and support she has been missing all her life. I love that I can give her this.

Thirty minutes later I can't take it anymore, and I make my way to Riley. My wife. I wrap my arm around her and whisper in her ear.

"It's time to go, baby, I can't take it anymore. I need you alone."

She smiles up at me and nods, so I take her hand and turn to my mom. "Sorry, but we are heading out," I say. Short sweet and to the point.

Mom laughs. "I'm surprised you lasted this long. Take care of her and my grandchild. See you in a week."

Suddenly I'm regretting inviting the family up to the lake house with us next week. I don't think I will get my fill of my girl in just a week. But I know Riley has been looking forward to having everyone come up and spend time with us, so I will do it for her.

Tonight, we are staying at a cabin on the property and heading out to Walker Lake, Texas tomorrow.

We walk out of the event barn hand in hand and I lead her to my truck. I make sure she has her seatbelt on, because, after all, she is carrying precious cargo. Then get in and head out to one of the cabins about ten minutes into the land.

"I don't think I've seen this cabin before?" Riley says as she stares out the window.

"This one has always been my favorite. My grandpa built it as a painting studio for my grandma. She loved to paint but said she needed different places to feel inspired. He knew we would need cabins eventually as the family expanded, so he built this one and gave each room a different theme. Come on I'll show you."

We walk in and I let her take a look around. It gives me a minute to take her in. She's a beauty in her wedding dress, like a glowing angel.

"The living room, dining room, and kitchen here all have a back to nature theme. My grandpa kept the wood cabin logs exposed with the stone fireplace, but he made sure the windows from the front of the house and the dining room area both had different views. You will see them in the morning, but the front of the house is all pasture and open fields. The back actually has a good view of the river off to the distance and a tree line. It's also where you can watch the Texas storms roll in. My grandma loved painting those."

I take her hand and lead her upstairs. "Up here each bedroom has a theme, let's see if you can guess it."

We walk into the first one which is easy. "Oh, it's a garden theme."

"Yep, my grandma painted that mural of the rose garden. She said because she saw nothing but flowers from this window."

The next room at first glance looks like a boy's room done up in blues.

"This one is either a sky theme or an ocean them."

"Close, a beach theme, the furnishings used to give it away most, but it's all packed up now. The third bedroom is a night-time room. Most nights you can see the moon from here. Come on, the master is downstairs and it's my favorite."

I carefully lead her downstairs to the bedroom off the living room.

"This was their retreat, where they would come to get away for a weekend."

"They were ahead of their times," Riley says as she looks around in awe.

This room is decorated in what we now call a farmhouse style and was my grandma's favorite.

"Eventually my mom and dad plan to move in here, and we will move into their place since we'll be running that side of the ranch. I'm guessing they will be making those plans sooner than we thought now."

I rub her belly and her eyes dance. I slowly walk behind her trailing my hand from her belly to hip and then up her back. I start to unlace her dress. It's an off the shoulder vintage gown that looks like it was made for her.

As I undo the last lace, the dress falls to the ground and she stands there in just a bra and thong.

"You are so beautiful," I whisper.

She smiles, steps out of her dress and runs her hands down my chest.

"And you have too many clothes on." She helps me remove my jacket, shirt, and pants until I'm standing there in nothing but my boxer briefs. I skim my hands down her sides, over her bare skin, taking in how she feels against me.

"Go lay on the bed, beautiful girl. You've given me two of the best gifts today, let me take care of you."

Soon as she is laying down, I remove her underwear. I don't even wait before my mouth is on her, lapping up her cream and latching onto her clit. I could live down here and die a happy man.

Just as she is on the verge of an orgasm, I start to kiss my way back up her belly and stop where our little peanut is.

"Hey, little one. I want you to know I love you and I am going to take such good care of you and Mommy. You are going to be born into the most amazing family and be so spoiled."

I continue kissing my way up to Riley's mouth. Tears glisten in her eyes as I kiss her mouth and position myself over her, sliding myself home.

She cries out my name as I pick up the pace. I can tell she is close as I am. Her walls flutter and clamp down on me.

"I love you, Riley with everything I am. I love you and will always protect you and our child, with my last breath. Thank you for this amazing gift."

It sets her over the edge, and she screams out her release and I follow right after her. I keep my weight off her as we catch our breath.

"Blaze, don't you know you gave me the best gift of all? Safety and family. Nothing I can ever give you will top that."

# Chapter 3

## Sage

*Sage*

*There were some days I didn't think we would ever get here.*

*Some days my heart bled that I might have ruined this chance.*

*Some days I still had hope.*

*I'm so glad I had hope.*

*Today I get to marry my soul mate.*

*Colt*

We have been through so much. It was easier as kids, it was pure. As adults it is hard. We've had a lot of insecurities to work through, but we are finally here.

I look at myself in my wedding dress and can't help but smile. Colt doesn't know but this dress is one his mom picked out, well kind of. She took me shopping once and we saw a wedding dress in a shop window just like this one. I still remember clear as day when she turned to me and said, "If I were to ever get married again, I'd get a dress like that." The look on her face was one of pure happiness.

It was a vintage style lace dress and I have pictured her wearing it hundreds of times.

I remember going home that night and looking up the dress and saving it. Growing up I knew two things about what my wedding might be like. I wanted this dress, and for it to be at the ranch church.

My wedding will be the first one at the church since Mom and Dad's wedding thirty years ago. Pastor Greg is so excited to marry us there. He loves the history of the building just like my family does.

I'm pulled from my thoughts as my phone goes off and I smile. Colt has been texting me all day.

**Colt:** 1 more hour...

**Sage:** 4 more hours until our wedding night...

**Colt:** Don't play dirty

**Sage:** I would never

**Colt:** I love you.

**Sage:** I love you too. I will be there, no doubts, no cold feet.

I know that's his biggest worry even if he won't admit it. He is worried I will panic and run again. I'm pretty sure it's why no one has left me alone, not even to pee, today.

What he doesn't understand is I've never been surer of him, or anything, in my life as I am today.

I also know that he is missing his mom, so I have found small ways of including her, like this dress and an empty seat in the front row. We've also used her favorite flower, blue princess verbena, everywhere today. My bridesmaid's dresses are also her favorite color, a dark teal.

Megan comes over to finish up my hair and makeup, and before I know it pictures are being taken and we are heading outside.

"Just got word the guys are at the church, it's time for us to head over," Riley squeals. She's taken over a lot of the organizing for me. She has a real knack for planning like my mom does. I know she is already helping Megan and Hunter plan their wedding as well.

We take several trucks over to the church and as we get out, I stop Riley.

"Riley go tell him I'm here. I know he's worried."

Her face softens and she nods and heads into the church. A minute later Dad comes out and everyone else heads inside.

"That boy was about to lose his mind before Riley popped in." Dad shakes his head and smiles.

"I know he's worried, but I have never been more certain of anything in my life."

"Good." He stands and stares at the church. "I never thought Blaze would be the first to get married. I always thought it would be you and Colt. You two didn't hide it as well as you thought. I always knew about you two. I thought you'd want to get married right out of high school and I was prepared to bargain and bribe you to wait until after college. Then you took off. I know the details now, but not stepping in was the hardest thing I ever had to do as a parent. I had many nights of TV dinners as your mother and I fought over it." He laughs.

"I had no idea you knew."

"Yep. I'm glad we are here now, and that you guys fixed it. Anyone with eyes can tell you two are meant to be. Now let's get in there before he comes out and throws you over his shoulder and carries you down the aisle. I think it's a real possibility."

I laugh as we head up the church steps and step inside the first set of double doors.

"Ready?" Dad asks. I take a deep breath and nod. He opens the next door and we start down the aisle.

The church takes my breath away with the blue flowers lining the aisle along with lanterns giving a soft glow.

My eyes sweep the church which is filled with so many of the friends I made while I traveled, all of them here to support me now. We invited pretty much the whole town, even Kelli who politely declined the invitation.

Then my eyes land on Colt. I've only taken 2 steps into the church and the emotion on his face causes my eyes to tear up.

Written on his face is so much love and emotion. This is the man who knew at such a young age that we would end up here today. This is the man who was by my side as I lay in hospital, both times, and never for a moment thought of leaving. This is the man who had walls up for everyone else but let them all down for me.

Our eyes lock and nothing else matters, no one else exists. By the time I am standing in front of him, he has tears running down his face. He doesn't even try to hide them.

I reach up and try to smile as I wipe them away. He covers my hand with his.

"We made it," he whispers.

"We made it," I whisper back.

He holds my hand the whole time, I think we both need the connection. The service and the vows fly by. By the time we are placing the rings on each other's fingers, we are both in tears again.

Colt barely waits for Pastor Greg to finish saying, "You may kiss the bride," before his lips are on mine; intense and short. Then he pulls back and leads me back down the aisle.

We decided after the ceremony we'd head to his mom's grave and spend some time with her before the photos. That's where we head next. Mom told me she was coming out here to decorate the headstone for the wedding, but Colt doesn't know that, so as we walk through the gate, he is wiping tears from his eyes.

"Mom wanted her to be involved. So did I."

"You did amazing with the colors and flowers." He nods.

I smile. "And the dress."

He looks me over before asking, "What do you mean?"

So, I tell him the story of his mom and me shopping and by the end, he is full on crying. It breaks my heart. I wrap him in a hug.

"I miss her too, but I know that of all days she wouldn't want you to be crying it's on this one."

"I know." He wipes his eyes and we stay and talk for a bit before heading back up to get photos done.

As we head into the reception he leans into my ear. "I will give you two hours tops before I toss you over my shoulder and carry you out of here."

I laugh because I don't doubt it for one minute. We are spending the night in our cabin before heading out on our honeymoon. Colt made me a promise to check things off my bucket list every year and he is starting with our honeymoon. I can't wait.

# Chapter 4

I made Sage a promise that I'd travel with her and help her finish checking off her bucket list and so far, we are doing a great job. We climbed Angel's Landing in Zion National Park. It was on Sage's bucket list, but she'd always been scared to do it. It was a scary hike, in places you have to hold onto a metal chain to keep your balance and not fall hundreds of feet to your death.

Scary as hell, but an amazing feeling to reach the summit together. The view from the top and the look on her face when we made it was all worth it.

I also took her to California and rented a convertible. We drove the Pacific Coast

Highway all the way to Seattle, making stops along the way for anything that caught her eye. The views along the coast were breathtaking and we spent a lot of time just sitting and staring at the water.

We are now at the last destination of our honeymoon in a cabin at Grand Teton National Park, her favorite place of all her travels. She wanted to share it with me, and as I stand here taking in the Tetons, I have to agree that they are breathtakingly beautiful, but they can't top the girl standing next to me.

Today we are driving the park loop trail and taking in the sites.

"There is just something so calming about this place. It was here I realized I didn't care what happened after I left and that I was heading home. I was going to fight for you. A week later Blaze met me at the Grand Canyon and then we got the call my land had gone up for sale. When I looked up again, two years had passed, and it felt like there was this huge wall between us."

"I know what you mean. We all threw ourselves into that land, but at any point, if you had walked up to me and said you wanted another chance; I'd have dropped everything."

"I know that now, but I was so scared you were just done with me. It took Riley to bring us back together."

I stand behind her and wrap my arms around her waist and hold her to me. "It did and I am so grateful to her for that."

We spend the rest of the day doing the sites along the drive making sure we hit all the famous ones like Mormon Row. We take so many photos and in true Sage style she makes friends everywhere she goes.

We get lucky and see both bear and bison on our drive before we head to the dinner reservations we have. This is where Sage introduces me to all things huckleberry which is a big thing around here. They look like blueberries but taste amazing and like nothing I have ever had before.

We head back to our cabin and cuddle up on the bed, just talking about the day and making plans to drive up to check out parts of Jackson Lake tomorrow. I love holding her in my arms like this, but I know it won't last long. Any time we get near a bed Sage is all over me like she is trying to make up for the lost time.

Sure, enough the second there is a lull in the conversation she rolls over and is straddling my hips and smiling down at me.

"Did I not satisfy you enough this morning, wife?" I run my hand up her side, taking her in.

"That was over nine hours ago." She pouts and grinds down on my cock.

"Anything you want, my love, always."

"I want you naked." She grins as she stands up. We both remove our clothes in record time, and then I'm lying back on the bed, with my hard cock jutting up into the air ready for her.

I can tell tonight is a night she wants to be in control, and I love giving her that to her. I watch her crawl up the bed between my legs and pause to give my cock a long slow lick. It takes everything in me not to try to thrust into her mouth.

When her eyes meet mine and she licks again I can't help the strangled groan that leaves me. It makes her smile before she sucks just the tip into her mouth. I grip the sheets trying not to grab her. Thankfully she has mercy on me and climbs up me to straddle my hips again.

She hovers just above the tip of my cock and locks eyes with me. Without breaking eye contact she slowly slides down my cock, slowly and steadily, while never once do her eyes leave mine. No words are spoken but at the same time, everything is said.

Sex with Sage has always been mind-blowing, but sex with my wife is on a whole other level. Knowing she is mine, seeing my ring on her finger, it does something to me. I've waited a long time to be here, and I'm enjoying the ride. Literally right now.

Sage leans down and kisses me. Her hard nipples slide against my chest, and her soft lips on mine are more than I can take. I grab her hips and slam up into her causing her to gasp and cry out my name.

"I love you, Sage and every day I need you more and more. I will never get enough of this. Not ever."

"Colt! God, I love you so damn much." She holds on to my shoulders as I tighten my grip on her hips and slam her down on my cock. Two more thrusts and my hot come is coating her deep inside and setting off her own orgasm making her scream my name.

There is nothing like knowing you were able to give your woman that kind of pleasure or to fall asleep with her on your chest and your cock buried deep inside her.

# Chapter 5

My family thinks I was nervous when I had a bridesmaid cancel on me last minute. Nope, I knew it was fate. I was able to ask Ella to step in and stand with Jason. She is going to be my sister soon so it's perfect.

When Jason came to the family a few weeks ago saying he wanted to ask Ella to marry him I jumped in and told him he should do it at my wedding. They met in the event barn so what better place to propose.

He loved the idea and it was easy to get Hunter on board. Us girls have come up with a brilliant plan for him to propose during my flower toss. It's taking everything in me not to give it away while I'm getting ready today.

Ella's family have jumped into helping with the wedding head on, and I have to say, I never expected to feel this kind of peace on my big day. But then I'm marrying my best friend after all.

I find it funny when Riley and Sage both disappear, knowing that their guys are going crazy not being able to see them just like I'm sure Hunter is.

Speaking of Hunter... his mom bursts through the door.

"Megan honey, we need to make sure you have your something old, something new, something borrowed, and something blue."

By the look on my mom's face, I know they have been planning something.

"Okay?" I say hesitantly.

"Well, this necklace has been worn by every bride in my family for generations. I don't have a daughter, so I'd be honored to pass it down to you. This qualifies as your something old, and blue," Donna says.

I take in the beautiful antique necklace with a sapphire heart in the center. It's a showstopper and I can't believe I get to wear it.

"It gets passed on to your oldest daughter when the day comes." Donna winks.

Sage steps up next. "This is your something new it's from your soon to be hubby."

I open the box and find a tiny wedding cake charm. I can't help but smile as I add it to my bracelet.

"I have your something borrowed." Mom holds her hand out and in it are her diamond dangle earrings Daddy got her for their 20th wedding anniversary that I've always loved. "Just make sure I get them back." She gives me her stern Mom glare.

Jill helps finish my hair and makeup before we head out to take some photos. I wanted to have a real country wedding, so even though we are getting married in the ranch church, I wanted a lot of the barn and horse wedding photos.

We decided to use the barn on this side of the property. The girls are in coral pink knee length dresses and are all wearing cowgirl boots. Even I have cowgirl boots on, I managed to find a white pair that have stitching that is the same color as the girl's bridesmaids' dresses.

We get some photos near the barn, some with the horses in the background and even one with cowboy hats on. We are having so much fun, time flies right by because the next thing I know Riley is saying it's time to head to the church.

"Blaze says Hunter is in the church and he is getting everyone in their places." Riley goes on about the order of who is going down the aisle, but I just tune her out and smile as my eyes land on my dad waiting outside for me.

I pictured this day many times growing up. I knew I wanted to get married at the church like mom and dad, and for a long time, it was to a faceless groom. Once I met Hunter it was always his face at the end of the aisle even when I swore we were just friends.

Everyone heads inside leaving me alone with dad for a few minutes.

"I've been looking forward to this day just as much as I have been dreading it. I'm so happy it's Hunter you are marrying, but it doesn't make giving away my little girl any easier."

"I love you, Daddy. I'm not leaving the ranch, nothing is changing but my last name."

"Yet that feels like everything."

Riley peeks her head out. "You're up!"

We smile and make our way into the church. As we start our way up the aisle, I can't stop the smile that crosses my face. I chose to have the couples stand together across the stage instead of guys on one side and girls on the other and it's perfect.

Blaze is standing behind Riley with his hands over her tiny baby bump. Colt is standing behind Sage the same way, but their hands are locked together. Jason is standing next to Ella with her hand resting on his arm and Mac and Jill are standing together both looking a bit awkward but still smiling and talking to each other. I send up a silent prayer Mac will find the girl for him and soon; I want him happy.

Then my eyes land on Hunter. There is so much emotion on his face, but he has a huge smile there too. He held out hope for this day for so long. He was strong for us and I really believe he is the reason we are here today.

Some days I wish I'd opened my eyes and seen him as more than a friend sooner. Other day's I'm glad it played out the exact way it did. Everything happening on the road trip the way it did was perfect.

Speaking of road trips, he has another one planned for our honeymoon and has told me it's back to Arizona but not Sedona.

My dad hands me off to Hunter who takes both my hands and doesn't let go for the whole ceremony. Hunter talked me into writing our own vows and now I'm thinking I need to thank Jill for the waterproof make up.

"Hunter, I had no idea the impact you would have in my life the day we met. I'm glad you got ditched on that date, I'm glad you came home for dinner with me that night. Over the last few weeks, I've thought about how different our story would have been if I'd opened my eyes sooner, but I always come to the same conclusion, I love our love story. So today I stand before all our family and friends and I promise to always talk to you. I won't ever walk away again, even if it means throwing a loaf of bread at you instead." Mom and Dad laugh harder than anyone at that one. Hunter's face is pure happiness, so I keep going.

"I promise to always support you and be by your side, to love you and show you how much I love you daily. I promise to let you bring home as many wounded animals that need homes as we can hold. Just not the snakes, I draw the line at snakes. I promise someday soon to start a family with you because I can't wait to see you as a dad. And I promise when we are old and gray, to sit next to you on the front porch watching our grandkids and telling them the story of how we fell in love."

There are several 'awes' from around the church before Hunter starts.

"I guess I should start this with a confession. The cheerleader who stood me up that night was Mandy Evans. I ran into her in town a few years ago. I thanked her for standing me up because I got to meet you. I'm telling you this because if it hadn't been for her, we wouldn't be here today. I remember knocking on her door and being pissed she wasn't home. Then I turned around and bam, there you were. From the moment I heard your voice, I knew we would be here today. Today I promise you my love, loyalty, friendship, and protection. I promise you will always come first. I know your dream was to own the beauty shop and you did that all on your own, but any other dreams you have, I promise to help them come true. I promise to spend every day for the rest of my life making sure you are happy and know how much I love you, because without you, Megan, I'm not me."

Stupid tears run down my face. We exchange rings and Hunter doesn't even wait for us to be announced husband and wife before his lips are on mine. It's a sweet kiss with a promise of more to come. As he pulls back, he whispers against my lips.

"I love you, my wife."

I smile and whisper back, "And I love you, my husband."

# Chapter 6

It's been three amazing days of having Megan as my wife. We spent the first forty-eight hours locked in the cabin I rented, and not once did we put on a bit of clothing. Of course, that led to me always being hard.

Naked Megan cooking, naked Megan watching TV, naked Megan taking a shower, you get the idea.

Today we are actually getting out of the house. I chose Tucson Arizona for our honeymoon for a few reasons. One is we can visit Saguaro National Park, try the food here, and the biggest reason is because of today.

Today we head down to Tombstone, Arizona. We are both excited about this trip. She loves the history of it all and I love it because I grew up watching old westerns with my dad.

We pull into downtown and Megan's eyes shine with excitement as we walk down the historical main street.

"So, what do you want to do first?" I ask as I watch her take it all in.

"Let's see what time the shootout re-enactment is and plan that first!"

We get our tickets for just after lunch and decide to walk the shops and tour Wyatt Earp's house before eating at one of the saloons in town.

We watch the shootout re-enactment, seeing her get into it as much as I do, is an amazing feeling. When we get back onto the street there's one of those old stagecoaches that give tours around town, so we jumped in and I get to hold her in my arms for an hour while we get an amazing tour of the town and learn so much history.

Next is the courthouse museum followed by the Boot Hill graveyard as the sun is setting.

Megan gets pictures of the graveyard but all of mine are of her as the desert sunset light hits her and gives her a glow like nothing I have ever seen.

We get back to our little cabin that night after grabbing dinner.

"I think we need to take a bath in that jacuzzi tub." There's a glint in her eyes as she turns. She makes her way to the bathroom removing her clothes as she goes, knowing she's driving me crazy.

By the time the water is warm, I am hard as hell watching her fix the bath naked. I get in and slide against the back and pull her to sit between my legs.

"Such a great way to relax," she says with a moan. I grab the washcloth and put some of her soap on it and start to wash her and I rub her shoulders and her arms. She rests her head back on my shoulder and I wash her breasts and play with them under the water as her nipples harden.

Then I wash down her belly teasing and avoiding her core. I wash her legs before my fingers find her clit at the end of their journey traveling back up her thighs.

She gaps and rolls her head to the side as I start strumming her hard nub and insert two fingers deep inside her.

"Hunter!" She gasps. I pull my hand away and she lets out the sexiest whimper.

"Get on your knees, put your hands on the edge of the tub in front of you, ass in the air."

She quickly moves into position and it is such a damn turn on that she trusts me and listens to what I ask.

I get on my knees behind her and run a hand up her back, holding her hips in place as I slide into her causing us both to moan.

"I got used to having you all day, but then today I had you in my arms for eight hours before I could get my cock back into you. This trip is ruining me, how will I handle 12 hour days back home?" I thrust in and out as I lean over her.

"We will have to get creative." She moans low and loud.

"The whole town will know that I'm taking you in your office on your lunch break every day. There won't be any hiding it."

Feeling her pussy clamp down proves she loves my dirty talk.

"You like the idea of that baby?" I whisper in her ear, then bite her ear lobe causing her to moan again.

"We will make it a daily thing. Everyone in town will know what happens during lunch. Maybe I'll have you come to the clinic, on the days my dad isn't there, and take you in my office again."

She gasps my name and falls over the edge so fast with no warning that when her pussy clamps down on me I start to come so hard it starts dripping out of her and down my balls.

After a minute a laugh. "God, Megs I love you. Now we need a shower to clean off."

We both laugh and drain the tub and head in for a quick shower.

Later that night when we are lying in bed Megan shocks the hell out of me. "I know we just got married but how long do you want to wait before we have kids?"

I smile. "I'd be happy if you were pregnant today, but I'd be happy to wait a few years too. I'll leave that choice up to you and the Good Lord."

We fall asleep that night talking about kids, and names we like and don't like things we want to do as a family. Family vacations and photos, and how we can't wait for them to grow up on the ranch.

Picturing little versions of Megan running around is enough to make my heart happier than it's ever been.

# Chapter 7

It didn't take everyone long to fix the little bit of mess Seth made in the church and now looking around you'd never know he was here. Perfect. I'd have rather not told Ella, but after her confronting me last night in her room, I knew she wouldn't go for that.

All the guys are at Mom and Dad's house getting dressed, and it's been great having them around. I'm in my old room and I take a look around and realize it was a really weird time for me. I was working at WJ's and into all things Iron Man and trucks.

I remember my senior year of high school Dad took me to Dallas for a monster truck show and it was a whole weekend just him and I. I found out then I got my love of trucks from him. My love for the color red might have come from my Iron Man days though.

I smile. You can't beat an old truck with a bench seat where you can pull your girl close as you are driving down the road.

There is a knock on the door and Blaze peeks his head in.

"Hey, man. Riley is texting for us to get down to the church."

I smile. Show time. Just as I'm stepping out the door to head to the church my phone goes off.

**Ella**: I don't want our first kiss to be in front of everyone! What were we thinking?
**Me**: Then it won't be. Trust me?
**Ella**: Always.
**Me**: See you soon, sweetheart.

I can't keep the smile off my face. I will kiss her anywhere but knowing she is thinking about it, grips my heart. Knowing it will be a moment just between us is perfect. My mind starts racing with ideas.

We get to the church and I take my place at the end of the aisle with Pastor Greg.

"Hey there, Jason. You ready for today?"

"Pastor Greg all due respect, I'm so damn ready I think I'd crawl out of my skin if I had to wait another day."

He laughs at that. The kind of laugh that fills the church and has a way of calming my nerves. He's a great guy and I can see why the church ladies try to push every single girl in town his way. He's going to make a great husband one day.

Then the music changes and couples start walking down the aisle. Ella decided to have the couples stand together just like Megan did. I think that's more for Royce's benefit though.

Royce walks in first with Anna Mae on his arm and a beaming smile. They both seem happy and I think someday soon we will be at their wedding.

Next are Hunter and Megan. They have this dreamy look on their face, no doubt reliving their wedding here just a month ago.

Then comes Sage and Colt both with big smiles. Those two have been so much happier since they found their way back to each other.

Riley and Blaze follow, and her baby bump is on full display. Blaze loves showing it off and really, I can't blame him. It's a huge way to say this girl is mine. Riley just glows and you can't beat that.

Maggie and Mac follow. They are the last couple coming up the aisle. Mac has been distracted lately. I think he's met someone, but he won't talk about it.

I tried to get Nick to stand up with me, but he said he'd be more honored if I let him handle the food for the wedding, and of course, I agreed. I think it was his way of getting out of wearing a suit.

The music changes again and my eyes lock on the door of the church, knowing that my angel is about to step through. The next moment there she is on her dad's arm, all dressed in white. Everything is perfect.

Her eyes lock with mine and I know my smile has to be as big as hers. With each step she takes toward me the emotion of the day hits me hard and I have to look at my feet for a moment to get them in check.

It does no good because when I look back up at her again, I can't stop the tears filling my eyes. She is so beautiful. I've waited so long for her, for this moment—for it to finally be here is overwhelming.

My eyes never leave hers, and as she makes the final steps toward me, I lose the battle and my tears start to fall. She reaches up and wipes away the tears from my eyes.

"I love you, Ella," I whisper.

"I love you too, Jason," she whispers back. We are in our own little bubble until someone clears their throat and it earns a few chuckles from our family and friends.

The service continues but I can't take my eyes off of her. She is absolutely glowing today and her eyes sparkle. She is too good for me, too perfect, and I am just so damn lucky she chose me.

After we exchange our rings, I can tell she is getting nervous again. I give her hand a squeeze.

"Don't worry, sweetheart."

She offers me a trusting smile and as Pastor Greg announces us as husband and wife I smile and lean in to kiss the top of her forehead. As whispers start around the church, I turn to them and smile.

"Sorry folks. Our first kiss isn't for public eyes." Then I pick her up and carry her out of the church to my truck.

This first kiss has me more nervous than my first kiss at that football game in 8th grade. Knowing she has waited her whole life for this kiss; I know I have to make it right by her.

"Where are we going?" she asks as we make out way down the driveway.

I smile. "Somewhere we can be alone for a few minutes. Come on."

I pull her into the barn office and take a minute to just take her in.

"Ella, Ella, Ella," I sigh. "This dress looks amazing on you. You're so beautiful, so perfect, and so mine." I bring a hand up to her cheek and run my thumb over her bottom lip enjoying how soft it is before slowly moving my hand around to the back of her neck. I rest my other hand on her hip and lower my head just a bit.

I search her eyes. For what I'm not sure, but the certainty there takes my breath away. I pull her so the front of her body is against mine with no space between us. When her head tilts back to look at me I slowly start to close the distance between her mouth and mine. I move slowly, allowing her to stop me at any point, but thankful she doesn't.

When her lips finally meet mine it's like the world stops moving and everything seems right in my life. This first kiss is soft and sweet, just getting to enjoy the feeling of her lips on mine, getting to taste her for the first time.

This simple kiss has me more turned on than anything ever has. My heart is racing and I'm so hard I'm worried I might scare her off, but I need her closer. I wrap one arm around her lower back pulling her in and tilting her head back to deepen the kiss.

I can't stop the moan that escapes me as I spin her around and press her back against the door, which earns me a gasp from her. I slide my tongue into her mouth and pin her to the door as she wraps her arms around my neck.

I cup her face and start kissing down her jaw and her neck to a spot just below her ear. I run my teeth across her skin and smile as her body shivers and she lets out a small moan.

My hands glide down her body as I grip her ass and hold her tight grinding into her just a bit so she can see what she does to me. As her hands slide down my chest, I know she wants to get her hand on my cock, but I won't take her here, we still have photos and a reception to get to.

I take her hands in mine and pin them to the door above her head and rest my forehead on hers.

"I don't want to leave this room. I don't want to stop kissing you, and I don't want you to take your hands off me. But your first time won't be here like this and if we keep going, I won't be able to stop."

She nods her head as she tried to catch her breath. I pull back just enough to look into her eyes.

"That was one hell of a first kiss, Ella. I knew it would be good between us. I just never dreamed it could be this good."

"Me either," she whispers.

I wrap my arms around her and hold her tight.

My wife.

My everything.

# Chapter 8

## Ella

Married life is amazing. I can't describe the feeling of waking up next to Jason every morning. Well, maybe I can, orgasmic.

He wakes me up every morning with an orgasm and what girl would complain about that? I think it's the perfect way to start your day.

But today is different. Today I happen to be up before him, and I smile. Time to flip the tables. I carefully move down the bed, pulling the sheet with me toward his already semi hard cock.

I don't have much experience with cocks, or any experience with anything really. But I can tell you Jason's is amazing; it looks beautiful and feels amazing when it stretches me.

I look back up at Jason who is still sleeping and then I lean down and gently place my hand at the base and slide the head into my mouth. It just takes one slide in my mouth and he's already thickening and getting harder.

One more slide in and out and he's hard and starting to stir. I pick up the pace a bit as he wakes up with a loud groan. I'm watching him as I work him in and out of my mouth and the moment his eyes pop open and he sees me his eyes go wide and the next second he tosses his head back and throws an arm over his eyes.

"Fuck! Oh, fuck, sweetheart, your mouth is heaven." He moves his free hand into my hair but doesn't try to stop me.

"Sweetheart, I'm going to come, and I want to come inside you." He starts trying to pull me toward him, but we aren't having that today. I grip his balls in one hand and suck harder as I take in even more of him.

His abs tense and he groans out a very strained, "Ella!" Then his hot come coats the back of my throat and I swallow down every drop before I pull back and give the head of his cock a kiss.

He pulls me up to lay on his chest, wrapping both arms around me and holding me tight.

"Holy hell, sweetheart, that is one hell of a way to wake up."

I giggle. "That's how I feel every morning."

"Then I guess I know what I'm doing every morning for the rest of my life." Before I can answer he flips me over and pulls my legs apart so he can settle between them.

"Now it's breakfast time." He smiles before he sucks on my clit. My hand flies to his head.

"Baby you are so soaked; it's running down your thighs. Did having my cock in your mouth cause this?"

"Yes," I moan.

He licks up my cream while moaning. "Guess we will have to have it there more often then."

His mouth sucks on my clit again as he slides two fingers into me and curls them.

"Already so close," he continues sucking on my clit again.

I am so close I can't even answer him as my hips start to buck trying to get closer, to get more pressure. I feel him smile before he nips lightly at the bud of nerves which sends me crashing over screaming his name.

"My favorite breakfast," he murmurs as he kisses his way up to my mouth. I can barely move which makes him smile.

"Now it's time for me to feed you. Stay here sweetheart, let me take care of you."

I nod and roll over to cuddle with his pillow as he brings the blanket up to cover me.

Before I know it the smell of coffee and bacon fills the house and Jason brings in a tray of food for us. We spend the morning in bed eating and talking about anything and everything. He always wants to know about my childhood, school, friends, and anything else. He says it's because he wants to know every part of me.

After lunch, I notice the sun shining outside and decide it's time we leave the house a bit.

"I think I'm going to go change and layout on deck." I smile at him.

He leans over and kisses my cheek. "Okay, I'm going to clean up in here and call Mom and Dad to see when they will be here this weekend. Then I'll join you."

I nod and head into the bedroom. Perfect. One of the things I bought on my sister girl's trip to Dallas before the wedding was a swimsuit. Well, I bought two of them. One for while I'm around other people. It's a one piece in a 1950's vintage style with a high neckline and shorts.

The other bathing suit is the one I'm going to put on now. It's for when it's only Jason and me and it's a bikini. I've never worn a bikini a day in my life, but I thought it would be a fun surprise for Jason. I quickly get dressed and then wrap a towel around me. As I'm leaving the room Jason comes in with the phone to his ear. He kisses my temple as he walks by and I head out to the deck.

I pick a lounge chair to the side of the deck that is still in the sun, but hidden from the lake should anyone go past. I recline the chair so I can lay down and get comfortable. As the sun warms my skin, I close my eyes and lose track of time, and just enjoy how calm everything is.

Next thing I know a finger is tracing the top triangles of my bikini.

"What exactly are you wearing, sweetheart?"

I smile not even needing to open my eyes.

"You don't like my bathing suit?"

"I fucking love your bathing suit, so will any other male who sees it."

I fake pout. "But I love this bikini."

He growls and I smile for a brief second before he yanks the ties on my bikini bottoms, I barely get my eyes open before his body covers mine and he thrusts hard into me.

"This is what any man who sees you in this will try to do to you." He pulls out and trusts in again making me moan his name.

"They will line up to have their turn and not care that you are mine. I will have to kill every one of them and rip the eyes out of anyone who looks your way. Do you want their blood on your hands?"

He picks up the pace and leans down and pulls my breasts from the fabric, leaning in and biting my nipple, causing me to cry out.

"Answer me."

"No!" I gasp.

"That's right because you're mine." Thrust. "Only." Thrust. "Mine."

I dig my nails into his back, I've never seen this rougher side of Jason before but it's turning me on like I can't believe it.

"I'm yours, Jason. Only yours."

"Damn right you are." This time he pinches my clit and my orgasm crashes into me, he follows with just a few more thrusts.

He collapses on top of me and as we catch our breath I giggle.

"Guess it's a good thing this bikini is just for you. I have a modest one piece for when we are around other people.

"Thank fuck, because there is no way I can let you out in public wearing this. Even if you look sexy as hell."

I don't get much of a tan because Jason gets hard every time, he looks over at me in my pink bikini and after the 3rd time, we head inside and spend the rest of the day in bed.

# Chapter 9

## Sarah

When I was a little girl Sky and I would always play wedding days. We would switch who was the bride and who was the wedding planner. Her mom was great at playing along. She would make cake samples for us to taste and build a box of decorations for us to use.

Each wedding became an all-day thing. We would plan and do food and then get married to our favorite Ken or GI Joe Doll before dinner and dinner would be our reception. We loved making new themes and it was always elaborate.

Sky's mom would buy us bridal magazines and we'd plan the most elegant weddings. Weddings that I know today might run over a million dollars.

Not once did younger me think older me would want a simple wedding in a ranch church in the small town of Rock Springs, Texas to a sexy as hell cowboy. If I could only go back and share this story with my younger self, I know she wouldn't believe me.

I've traded the diamonds for glitter and twinkle lights and the silk for lace and burlap. Who knew?

The best part is the sexy cowboy who will be waiting at the end of the aisle for me. From the moment I met him, his face was in every wedding fantasy I had. Today I get to make them come true.

I'm ready to get to the church and be Mac's wife. Time is going way too slow and Ella mistakes it for nerves.

"Oh, Sarah everything is going to be perfect." Ella hugs me.

"It will be, but thank goodness this is the last wedding for a while. At least Riley gave us four months to plan, but they've kept getting shorter and shorter after that. I need a vacation after doing this one in three weeks." Mac's mom laughs.

"It was easy, we had the decorations and everything ready to go, the hardest part was finding her dress." Riley waves her hand in the air like it was no big deal.

She is still on bed rest but Blaze is allowing her to be part of this, but she has to stay sitting always with her feet up as per doctor orders. I think she was just happy to have something to do and would have planned it in forty-eight hours if we'd have asked.

We knew we didn't want to wait long. We've been dancing around each other for the last seven years and are both ready to start our lives together, waiting any longer than necessary seemed pointless.

"You know he offered to take me to Vegas to elope, he didn't even want to wait this long." I laugh.

"That boy had better have thought to invite his family! I swear I wish I'd thought of a Vegas wedding for all of you.

I've always wanted to go." Helen laughs along with me.

"I heard Nick joke with Jason that he wants to do his bachelor party in Vegas if he ever gets married," Ella adds.

"Well, I liked how you all did a big family event for yours." Helen nods.

"What did you all do?" I ask them.

"We had a day down at the swimming hole with everyone. Did a cookout and everything." Riley smiles.

"Ours was a night of dancing at the bar with some of Nick's BBQ." Sage laughs. "Can't wait until the reception, I'm so glad you let him cook for your wedding!"

"We did a day in Dallas doing some laser tag and one of the escape rooms," Megan reminisces.

"We really didn't have one, what with everything going on." Ella shrugs. "I loved your game night one though."

I smile, we decided to do a huge game night and invite all our friends. There was a lot of food and drinks. We set up game stations around the house. There were video games, and board games, card games, and even Twister. The night ended with a surprise from Mac where he and the guys blew up this stair slide that went on the staircase and we all took turns sliding down and landing on a mattress at the bottom.

There is a knock on the door and a minute later Blaze walks in. His eyes scan the room until they land on Riley.

"The guys are at the church. You ready to head down?" he asks her.

It took some convincing to get him to allow Riley to be in the wedding but since there are stairs at the front of the church, we decided to have everyone sitting on them so Riley can keep her feet up.

Blaze carries Riley to his truck, and we all follow and head to the church.

"I think you have the largest wedding party out of all of us," Sage says when we pull up at the church.

"Yep, one more than me," Ella chips in.

I watch them all head in down the aisle. Blaze carries Riley which causes some laughs. Sage and Colt follow with Megan and Hunter behind them.

"Ready, sweetheart?" Jason asks Ella just before they take their turn down the aisle. Lilly and Mike are next, that one was Riley's idea, she's so sure there is something going on between the two. Jenna is parried with Mo; the tribe leader from the reservation Mac grew up on and they have been talking up a storm ever since she got into town a few days ago. She loves learning about the tribe.

Sky and Ben are the last couple to walk down. After Lee and my parents were locked up, Ben and Mac became fast friends. So, when we realized we needed one more groomsman Ben was the first-person Mac wanted to ask and Ben was thrilled to join us.

I'm so lost in thought I don't realize Tim, Mac's dad has walked up beside me. He offered to walk me down the aisle just like he did for Riley who also didn't have a father to walk her, of course, I took him up on it. He's always treated me like a daughter.

"Ready?"

"Been ready for the last five years." I smile and Tim laughs.

We make our way into the church and everything is perfect because at the end of the aisle is my cowboy standing in his cowboy formal with his boots and cowboy hat on. I've never seen him look sexier.

His eyes are fixed on me and his wide smile lights up his face. I feel like I am floating down the aisle to him. It's not until I am standing right in front of him that I notice the unshed tears in his eyes.

"Sunshine, you look stunning."

"You look pretty sexy there yourself, cowboy."

The ceremony flies by with the vows and ring exchange.

"I now pronounce you husband and wife. You may kiss the bride."

"You and me forever, Sunshine." Mac leans in.

"You and me forever, husband." I smile back.

Mac growls and leans in for one hell of a first kiss as husband and wife.

# Chapter 10

## Mac

I offered to take Sarah anywhere for our honeymoon. Paris, Italy, Bali. I mean anywhere. Where did she want to go? To the lake house.

She says our story started there and our marriage should too. You can't argue with that logic.

Once we got here, I asked her what she wanted to do, and she said she wanted to do all the things we normally do while here. It's a little too cold to go swimming but we have made plenty of use of the hot tub.

We've had a few warm days where she's laid out on the deck in a red bikini that looks a lot like the one I saw her in that first day. That's led to us role playing a very different version of our first meeting between us.

The colder weather is perfect for lighting up the fire pit at night, cooking smores, and just cuddling and talking.

Today Walker Lake is having a winter carnival downtown and we decided to spend the day there and pop into the diner to see Beth for dinner and then stick around to see the lighting of the town as they turn on the Christmas lights for the first time.

When she steps into the living room wearing a grey sweater dress with black leggings, boots, and a dark red scarf I realize this is the first time I have seen her like this. Normally it's summertime and she is always in warm weather clothes.

I shake my head and wrap my arms around her waist. "You look beautiful, Sunshine. Now let's get going before I drag you back to bed."

She laughs and drags me out to the car. We find parking pretty easily and walk into the town square where there are tents set up in rows with everything from food, to clothes, arts, and crafts, and even some games. We do some Christmas shopping and I run the bags back to the car just in time for the parade.

Walker Lake is a small town, but from what Sarah has told me, they love to celebrate Christmas. The parade is done up right with scenes from iconic Christmas movies, performances, and of course Santa and his reindeer at the end. With real reindeer.

"Where to now?" I ask.

"Now the rides!"

"I didn't see any rides?"

She drags me along behind her to an area just past the town square and it opens up with all kinds of rides you'd expect to see at any fair or carnival including a Ferris Wheel near the lake.

We spend a few hours riding rides and save the Ferris Wheel for last. Once we are seated and it starts to climb Sarah sighs.

"This is always my favorite part of the festival. I love the lights but there is something about getting to see the town and the lake from above. Normally Sky rides with me. I have to say the company is much better this year."

"You know it's good luck to get stopped at the top?"

"Oh, is it now?"

"Yep but it's bad luck if you don't kiss while you're stopped."

She laughs. "This sounds like something high school boys tell girls to cop a feel."

I laugh. "Maybe but I've never kissed anyone on the Ferris Wheel."

"Well I've only ever ridden with Sky and that would have been weird."

Then as luck would have it, we get stopped right at the top. Sarah looks over at me with a big smile and leans in for a kiss. I place my hand on the back of her neck and pull her to deepen the kiss. I don't pull away when we start moving again until we are back at the bottom.

"That was one hell of a good luck kiss, cowboy." She smiles as we exit and head toward the diner. The sun is starting to set so when we finish dinner it will be perfect for taking in the lights.

We walk in and the memories both good and bad rush over me. We had many more good times here and I try to hold on to them.

"Oh my gosh look at you two. Come over here and give an old woman a hug!" Beth yells across the diner as she rushes over to us.

"Mac good lord almighty you grew up good didn't you." Beth hugs me then stands back to look me over. "Wow Sarah good thing you locked him down! Even an old lady like me would 't be able to resist him otherwise!"

I'm pretty sure I'm blushing harder than I ever have in my life. Thankfully she turns her sights on Sarah.

"Look at you, you are positively radiant!" Beth hugs Sarah even harder than she did me. "Being married looks good on you! Now I have a table right over here. Anything you want tonight is on me. "

"Oh, Beth, thank you." Sarah hugs the woman right back.

"It's the least I can do to apologize about Lee. I had no idea. I feel like I should have known, and maybe I did, but I was so ready to retire that I turned a blind eye. I never thought he'd go after you..."

"Beth. It's okay. He's where he belongs and in a weird way, I think that's what pushed Mac and me together."

"Well, at least some good came out of it then. Now sit and let me feed you!"

We sit and watch the people out the front windows of the diner until Beth brings us our food.

"Oh, I want to tell you. My niece Austin decided she wanted to come and run the diner for me. She just got out of a bad relationship and was looking for a change. She has always loved visiting me here in Walker Lake, so she is really excited to move here. She is spending the holidays with her parents and then will be here mid-January."

"That's awesome, Beth! I met her a few times growing up she had so much energy and loved making people smile," Sarah says.

"Oh, she still does. She has such great energy that I think will fit in well around here. I gave her free rein to redecorate the place too, she wants to bring in more natural elements and highlight the lake."

"Oh, I love that idea I can't wait to see what she does with it! Gives us a reason to keep coming back." Sarah smiles over at me.

"Yes, it does." I kiss the tip of her nose then we dive into our food.

When we finish eating, we hug Beth and head out to check out the lights. The Mayor is just wrapping up his speech before he flips a switch and the whole square lights up.

There are lights strung over the road from the courthouse, over the street to the buildings on the other side making a lighted tent.

"I always love this. They close the square to traffic this time of year and put these lights up and have a bunch of events. Then at night, it's so much fun to walk under the lights." Sarah sighs and she leans against me.

"It really is magical."

We walk along the square then Sarah starts pulling me. "Come on I want to show you my favorite part of the lights."

I follow her down by the lake and the public dock has arches of lights covering it all the way to the end, so you are walking through a light tunnel.

"I've never seen anything like this, Sunshine."

"I love it. Come on I want to get our picture taken inside it."

We walk in and she takes a few photos of us and we just enjoy the lake and the lights you can see around the edge of the lake.

"The week before Christmas they offer boat tours of the lights along the lakeshore. I never went on one, it seemed so romantic. I wanted to do it with someone special."

"I wish we were staying, but I promise we will come back. Maybe next year we can talk the family into doing Christmas here and we can do the tour. You can give me the whole Walker Lake Christmas and New Years' experience."

"That would be perfect, Mac."

"Then that's what we will do, we will be back next year."

# Wedding Bonus Chapter

Tim and I have been empty nesters for a while now. Ever since the kids moved into Sage's side of the ranch. It's a different kind of empty nest though once the last of your babies get married.

Today we are having a big family dinner at my house, per Riley's request because she needs a change of scenery. Her due date is still about 6 weeks away, just after Christmas. The ranch has been hit with a huge snowstorm, so work has ground to a halt and they are all looking for something to do. I suggested we make an afternoon out of it and play some card games and maybe a movie night and everyone jumped on board. So today our house is filled, loud, and full of life.

I remember days when these kids were growing up and they were all running around and getting into trouble. Having six to look after, and with four of them being boys it was no easy task, but I loved every minute of it.

I am so proud of the adults they all have become. My family has now doubled in size and in a few short weeks my first grandbaby will be born, and number two will follow it in a few months. My heart is so full.

I look over at Blaze and Riley. He hasn't left her side, anything she needs or wants he is right there ready to get it for her. He's always had a protective caring streak in him, he proved that with how he was with Sage. For a while, there Tim and I thought Blaze and Sage would end up together, but Blaze and Riley are a perfect fit.

I watch him rub her stomach and play with their little one, they both have such huge smiles on their faces.

Earlier today Riley and Megan were talking and comparing first trimester stories. Riley was giving Megan tips and tricks to get her clothes to fit a bit longer. It was the exact kind of moment I always dreamed up for my kids.

Hunter hasn't left Megan's side either, making sure she is drinking enough water and eating often to keep her morning sickness away. I remember that night Megan brought him home. There was something between them, I could see it even then.

Megan kept him at arm's length, but I loved watching it develop, and knowing he had her back is a huge comfort to a mother. It didn't hurt that we were friends with his parents too.

Sage spent part of this morning in the kitchen with me making some desserts and helping me cook. Colt is never far behind where she is; he spent the morning talking with Tim about the ranch and about the last snowstorm we had here back when he was a kid.

Sage's just pulled the last of the biscuits out of the oven as Colt walks into the kitchen. He walks up behind her and wraps her in a hug and nuzzling her neck.

I still can't believe how long they hid things from us. I did have a few inklings there might be something between them during their senior year, but I never thought could be the reason why she left. When the story came out, a lot of things started to make sense, like the walks they were always talking, and when he always wanted to go into town with her on errands.

Then there are the newlyweds, well I guess they are all newlyweds since they've all been married in the last year. But I'm talking about Mac and Sarah, my newest bride and groom.

I'll never forget the look that crossed Mac's face that moment he saw Sarah. I knew. It was like after everything that he'd been through, he finally came alive. That summer when we left the lake house a shadow covered his face again and I knew. Of course, if I had known what was going with Sarah and her family, I'd have stepped in sooner.

Watching them now they are both so bright, happy, and full of life. They are cuddled on the couch watching a cooking competition show the girls all wanted to watch. Both Sarah and Mac look absolutely content and it warms a mother's heart.

That leaves my oldest, Jason. He was such a loner before Ella came alone. Never really dating but not seeming to miss it either. He threw himself into that bar and gave it everything he had. He turned it around and made it a family friendly place. It's really started to boom since the TV show aired and Tim and I couldn't be prouder of him.

All that said, Ella was the last person we ever pictured him with. There was a song out a while ago called *'Cowboys and Angels'* and that fits the two of them perfectly.

She is his angel, perfect, innocent light to his rough and tumble cowboy. They just fit.

Her family has fit right in too. They just moved to Rock Springs and brought Royce and Maggie with them. They are staying in the old family home on Sage's side of the ranch.

Poor Royce is still trying to get Anna Mae to give him the time of day. They talk and hang out, but she won't consider anything beyond that, but he soaks it up. Just like Hunter did. I told him to be patient, it will be key because she has to learn to trust again.

Now Maggie, she is starting to come out of her shell. She's a little spitfire and on a mission to find herself, she is going about it the right way too. She's still modest, but now wears jeans around the ranch and will go into town on her own. I've noticed the way she and Nick have been looking at each other. There is something there, it will boil over sooner or later.

Ella's parents fit right into Rock Springs. Her mom took a job in the church office and her dad fell into hire hauling. Sage had a client that needed help getting a horse to the ranch and well, Grant stepped right up and offered to go help pick the horse up. He was great and word of mouth spread, and he has been transporting a few horses a week. A few of Sage's clients prefer to pay him rather than do it themselves, so Sage offers it now in her packages.

Grant and Maria talked with us the other day and they decided to wait until this spring to look for a place in town. They aren't sure if they want something with a little bit of land or something in town. Sage told them to stay as long as they needed, and we agreed.

There is one more couple here tonight. Well, I guess they aren't an official couple because they are fighting it.

Lilly and Mike.

Now I'm not sure what is going on there, but the tension is high with Lilly being snowed in here and how much time she has been spending visiting Riley. I'm sure it won't be long before the spark ignites there.

The seasons in my life are turning. My time as a mother as I have known it is over and soon, I will be taking on a new name.

Grandma.

· · • • · • • • · ·

Read on about the family and see Blaze and Lily's child in **The Cowboy and His Mistletoe Kiss**

OR

Head over to Walker Lake and follow Jenna and Sky in **The Cowboy and His Beauty**

# More Books by Kaci M. Rose

**Rock Springs Texas Series**
The Cowboy and His Runaway – Blaze and Riley
The Cowboy and His Best Friend – Sage and Colt
The Cowboy and His Obsession – Megan and Hunter
The Cowboy and His Sweetheart – Jason and Ella
The Cowboy and His Secret – Mac and Sarah
Rock Springs Weddings Novella
Rock Springs Box Set 1-5 + Bonus Content

**Cowboys of Rock Springs**

The Cowboy and His Mistletoe Kiss – Lilly and Mike
The Cowboy and His Valentine – Maggie and Nick
The Cowboy and His Vegas Wedding – Royce and Anna
The Cowboy and His Angel – Abby and Greg
The Cowboy and His Christmas Rockstar – Savannah and Ford
The Cowboy and His Billionaire – Brice and Kayla

# Connect with Kaci M. Rose

Kaci M. Rose writes steamy small town cowboys. She also writes under Kaci Rose and there she writes wounded military heroes, giant mountain men, sexy rock stars, and even more there. Connect with her below!

**Website**
**Facebook**
**Kaci Rose Reader's Facebook Group**
**Goodreads**
**Book Bub**
**Join Kaci M. Rose's VIP List (Newsletter)**

# About Kaci M Rose

Kaci M Rose writes cowboy, hot and steamy cowboys set in all town anywhere you can find a cowboy.

She enjoys horseback riding and attending a rodeo where is always looking for inspiration.

Kaci grew on a small farm/ranch in Florida where they raised cattle and an orange grove. She learned to ride a four-wheeler instead of a bike (and to this day still can't ride a bike) and was driving a tractor before she could drive a car.

Kaci prefers the country to the city to this

day and is working to buy her own slice of land in the next year or two!

Kaci M Rose is the Cowboy Romance alter ego of Author Kaci Rose.

**See all of Kaci Rose's Books here.**

# Please Leave a Review!

I love to hear from my readers! Please **head over to your favorite store and leave a review** of what you thought of this book!

Made in the USA
Columbia, SC
23 September 2024